To Dean + Mary

Happy trails

Michael B W

A PALE HORSE PUBLICATION

CHIP COLFAX
FLYING DEPUTIES

MICHAEL B. WHALEN

For information contact: info@palehorsepublications.com
Cover Art by Michael Thomas
Cover design by Pale Horse Publications
Published by Pale Horse Publications
April 2021
10987654321

ACKNOWLEDGMENTS

My niece Dr. Anne Elsbree for help with editing and format.

Ross Jackson for all his help, like getting my computer unblocked, and just being a good guy.

CHAPTER ONE

Well hell, now that the trial was over and that redheaded s.o.b. was going to hang for killing my ma and pa, it was time for Becky and me to get back to the ranch. We had been gone almost a week and had been staying with the sheriff here in Prescott, who was also my father-in-law.

Becky's folks were great people. They were in the sheriff's office when he said, "Chip, been meaning to talk to you about becoming my deputy down your way. I could really use another one off toward Wickenburg. What'd you say?"

"Gosh Sheriff, we'll have to go back to your house and talk to Becky before I can answer that."

"Well let's go see what she has to say."

Back at the house, they found both women fixing dinner in the kitchen. "Becky, your pa has asked me to become his deputy, what do you think.?"

"I guess it would be okay, what could go wrong down our way, anyway?"

Chip and Becky had only been married about a year and always made their decisions together.

"Hey Pop, what if you need Chip in a hurry, how ya gonna get him?"

"Well I've been thinking and thinking, and I might have a solution. Have you ever heard of homing pigeons?"

Three people shook their heads in unison.

"No sir, what has a pigeon got to do with being a deputy?" Mrs. Arrowsmith asked?

"Well you see, there's these pigeons you keep in a coop. You feed, water and even talk to them and they'll come back to their coop every time. So, we put a coop on your ranch and one at the sheriff's station and train them to fly back and forth, it's almost instant communication. They have a small container strapped to their leg that you can put a message in, and in less than an hour you can get an order from, say the sheriff's office to your ranch. What do you think about that?"

"Wow, what an idea," said Chip.

"So, you want to be our new west side deputy?" asked the sheriff.

"I don't know, what do you think Becky?"

"Gosh Chip, nothing much happens out our way, so why not, if you want to, we can call them flying deputies."

"Okay Sheriff, we'll try it, though I don't know much about the ins and outs of the law."

"You'll do just fine, you know two things, right from wrong, and how to trail and capture a bad guy. About all you need to know right now. So, tomorrow, we'll get you sworn in at the office and pin a badge on you."

"Okay, we'll do it Sheriff, but we need to get back to the ranch tomorrow, so can we do it early?"

"Sure," said the sheriff, "And the county will throw in a salary of ten dollars a month and practice ammo."

"Fine, said Chip, we'll be ready."

CHAPTER TWO

Next morning, they all enjoyed a breakfast of eggs, bacon, toast and coffee, then Becky and Chip hitched up the team to their wagon and went to the sheriff's office.

"Well, here we are Dad, let's get started, because we need to stop at the general store and get our supplies."

"Okay Chip, raise your right hand and repeat after me, I do solemnly swear to uphold the laws of Yavapai county and the territory of Arizona, so help me God."

Chip did so, and the sheriff shook his hand and handed him a badge. "Chip you don't need to flash this around, the fewer people who know about this, the better."

"Yes sir, we'll keep it under our hats," replied Chip.

They spent about an hour in the general store and headed for the ranch with a wagon load of supplies.

When they got home, Clyde, their old friend and Chip's father's old mining partner, who had happened by just after the three rustlers had killed his ma and pa, and had agreed to stay on and help with the ranch, was really glad to see them. Of course he wanted to know all about the trial, and all the details of the sentence, and when was the hanging.

They explained everything as they unloaded the supplies, and swore him to secrecy about the homing pigeons and Chip now being a deputy of Yavapai county.

He was really surprised and very pleased. All he could say was, "hot dang, hot dang," over and over and over.

That night after supper, they sat around and talked about the new plans, where to build the pigeon coup so the travelers who stopped in wouldn't be any wiser. They decided to build it behind the cabin so Becky could see it from the window, but nobody else could.

Chip had brought the plans that the sheriff had given him to make the coup. Nothing fancy, but it would keep them warm and dry. They would start on it tomorrow with all the lumber they had left over from building the bunkhouse on the side of the barn, where Clyde stayed and the few travelers used when they needed to stay overnight or just to get out of the weather. Because, sometimes, the weather got pretty bad between Prescott and Wickenburg.

There wasn't much money to be made, but every dollar was a dollar more than they had before.

They charged a dollar for food, bunk and feed for their livestock.

CHAPTER THREE

It didn't take Chip and Clyde but a couple of days to make a nice home for the pigeons. They all stayed busy the next couple weeks waiting for the sheriff to bring the pigeons down from Prescott. What with moving the cattle to a new pasture, working the garden, doing all the odd jobs around the ranch, they were very anxious.

When the sheriff finally arrived, he had six beautiful birds for the ranch. They put them in the new coup and stood back and admired them for a few moments before anyone said anything, then the sheriff said, "there you go Chip, your own flock."

"But," Chip said, "How do we train them?"

"I've already acclimated them to their home at the sheriff's office, so they know where the home base is and now you will feed, water and even talk to them. That way they will know that this is their other home, then they will automatically know where to come back to."

"You know what Dad, we'll name them Flying Deputies, what do you think?"

Becky had all six named already, Katie, Jane, Jo, Annie, Daley, and Peggy. Wow, what a woman. You just knew she would keep an eagle eye on them.

The next couple weeks they flew them back and forth from the ranch to Prescott and all seemed to go as planned. "Well let's get on with the deputy job."

As the new birds came in from Prescott, Becky named them too. Two weeks later, Chip and Clyde were down at the barn when Becky came running and yelling, "Katie just landed with a note from my dad."

"Well let's see it," said Chip. She handed the message over. It read:

TWO MEN

ROBBED BANK, KILLED TELLER, ONE WHITE HORSE, ONE BLACK, HEADED YOUR WAY, BE CAREFUL, I'll BE ALONG LATER.

"Clyde, saddle my horse, Becky, sack me up some jerky and some cookies and maybe some coffee while I get my shootin' irons."

He grabbed the .44 yellow boy and leaned it by the door, then went to the chest in the bedroom, got out the belt and holster, a .44 caliber pistol and strapped the rig on. He took the sack of food and hung it on the saddle horn, gave Becky a big kiss, climbed on his best horse and headed for the gate. He swung over on the trail and headed towards Prescott. He knew a spot about two miles up the trail where he could lay an ambush for the two bad guys and they would never know he was there until he had the drop on them.

He hid his horse and settled in behind a big boulder and waited. It was getting dark and nothing was stirring, so he got the food sack and his serape and settled in. Along about midnight he decided they weren't coming, so he went to sleep knowing that his dog, Ellsworth, would keep a sharp eye for anything coming near their hiding spot. He woke at daybreak, grabbed some jerky, and got to thinking, "if they didn't come this way, where else could they go?"

He had heard about a lake called Granite Basin that was off to the north of the trail, he'd never been there, but it was worth checking out before giving up the hunt.

He headed up the trail toward Prescott, till he came on the side trail, there was a board sign that said, *Granite Basin 2 mile.* He swung on to it and headed North. The wind was out of the South, hitting him square in the back and that was why Ellsworth didn't alert him. The first shot took his hat off, he dived out of the saddle, hit the ground hard and jerked out his hand gun, meanwhile, more shots were pinging all around him, he heard his horse scream and go down, he cranked off a shot in the direction of the shooting and squirmed behind a boulder. He lay there for at least five minutes without any more firing coming his way. Then he heard the thrashing of horses being mounted and then came the sound of running horses, they faded away and he got to his feet, picked up his hat and examined it. Damn, another inch or so lower and he would have been dead. He then went to check on his horse, he had been hit twice, once in the shoulder, but it was only a flesh wound, but the other had smashed his front leg. Nothing to do but put him down, so he did. He pulled off the saddle with the yellow boy still in the scabbard.

He still had the serape on as he headed back up the trail toward Prescott, it didn't take long until he had to shuck it and tie it to the saddle. Four hours later, he trudged into town and headed to the sheriff's office. When he shoved open the door there sat the sheriff all bandaged up. Now he knew why he wasn't on the trail after the bank robbers with him.

After he told the sheriff what had happened on the trail, the sheriff told him that he'd been hit in the shoulder by them as they were riding out of town.

They sat looking at each other, both seemed to be in deep thought. Chip spoke first, "they were headed North the last I heard of them, so they will probably head for Kingman, I'll get another horse and head out in the morning."

"No, that won't do the trick, Kingman is in Mohave County, we have no authority up there."

"Well I'll just go as a bounty hunter then."

"No," said the sheriff. "I got another idea, the United States Circuit Judge is due in here tomorrow, we'll get you sworn in as a US Marshal and you'll be able to go anywhere in the country and chase bad guys, what do you think of that?"

"Wow, sounds like a good idea to me," said Chip. So the county bought Chip another horse, even better then the one he had lost, and they went to the sheriff's house and waited for the judge to come from Phoenix tomorrow. Before they left the office, they sent a homing pigeon to Becky so she would know and wouldn't be fretting about him, had a fine meal. The doc came by and redressed the sheriff's wound, then they all hit the hay, for a much needed rest.

CHAPTER FOUR

Next morning, the judge was on the noon stage, the sheriff explained the situation to him, he agreed and swore in Chip as a new deputy marshal, by this time it was getting late in the afternoon, so he decided to wait till tomorrow to start trailing the bad guys.

When he and Ellsworth got to Granite Lake they were very cautious, real sneaky like and eased in and took a good look around, found where they had camped, had cooked, had bedded down, and one of the horses had a shoe that was broken on the end. Chip would put that on the back burner for maybe, just maybe, later use. They lined out the trail and sure enough, it was headed North like he thought. The ground was high desert, so the sand was dry and that made tracking pretty easy for the first day. He found where they had made camp and he did the same. The next morning, he hit the trail at daylight and made good time all day. He found their next campsite and used it, like before, he wasn't gaining anything, he figured he was probably three days behind, so he doggedly kept up the pace for three more days, not seeing a soul in this harsh environment. As he got closer to what he thought was Kingman, the terrain changed to rock and then became mountainous. He did come across a small mining camp of six hardcore miners who fed him and said, "yes there had been two riders who had passed about a half mile to the East, but they hadn't stopped and they were riding a white and a black horse."

"Good, but that was three days ago," he hadn't closed the gap at all. Next morning, he saddled early and headed for Kingman, he'd gotten directions from the miners, so he headed straight in instead of tracking them all the way and losing precious time. When he got to Kingman, he went straight to the livery stable and stopped at the hitching rail. He looked around before he stepped off his horse, went around and pulled the yellow boy from its scabbard and sauntered into the livery. Inside, he found an old man bent over an anvil working on a horseshoe.

He looked up and said, "howdy mister," then took another look and said, "I mean Deputy, what can I do for you?"

"I was tracking a couple of men who robbed the bank in Prescott, one has a bad shoe on..."

He was interrupted by the old man, "yep, that's what I'm working on right here. Their horses are out back in the corral, and I think they're staying over to the hotel."

"Thank you oldtimer, now where is the sheriff's office?"

He was told just around the corner, he nodded and headed out the door.

CHAPTER FIVE

When he got to the office, he walked in and introduced himself to the sheriff, he felt kinda funny saying US Deputy Marshal for the first time. He explained the whole case for the sheriff and asked what his thoughts were. "Ya, they came in a couple days ago, they both had saddle bags and rifles. They was headed for the hotel last I seen. Wanna go and take them in?"

"Let me get a drink of water and we'll go over to the hotel and see if they're still around."

"Help yourself, fresh this morning, pumped it myself."

Chip took a couple big dippers full, said he was ready and they both headed for the hotel.

The sheriff said, "whoa, that's one of them coming down the other side of the street, probably headed for the livery stable, let's wait and see if the other one shows up."

They both ducked in the hardware store and looked out the window and watched until the first one was headed back to the hotel, "okay let's take this one now."

They stepped out in the street and just stood there until the badman was about forty feet away and Chip said, "Hold it right there cowboy, and don't move, you're under arrest."

The badman stopped in his tracks, "What the hell you mean under arrest, what for?"

"Murder and bank robbery and attempted murder of the sheriff of Yavaoai county, and the attempted murder of a deputy, now put your hands in the air and don't move."

He stood stock still for just a few seconds, then grabbed for his six shooter, he got it out and was bringing it to bear when Chip's yellow boy barked, the .44 slug took him right in the middle of his chest, knocking him back about ten feet against the building. He was dead before he hit the ground. Chip said to the sheriff, "Wish he hadn't done that."

CHAPTER SIX

When they went through the badman's pockets they found $94 dollars. "So they probably took a hundred bucks apiece for walking around money, now to find the other bad-guy, and find the rest of the bank's money." Chip put the money in his pocket. By this time a crowd was gathering, wanting to know what was going on. Then down the street a man was running and yelling, "he stole my horse, he stole my horse."

The sheriff asked him who stole his horse, he said he didn't know, but he headed South out of town. Another man ran up and told the sheriff it was one of those guys that rode in a couple days ago and was staying at the hotel.

Chip said to the sheriff, "we better check their room and see if he took the rest of the money with him."

By this time the undertaker who ran the lumberyard was looking at the dead guy, "well, who's gonna pay for this?"

Chip said, "take his horse, saddle and guns, that should be more than enough to fill the bill."

The sheriff asked Chip, "ready to check out the hotel?"

When they got to the room, it wasn't very tidy, but what would you expect, under the rumpled mattress they found the money all laid out in nice neat rows. When they counted it, they had $9,800 dollars, they grabbed one of the bandit's saddle bags, dumped out the dirty clothes and put the money in.

Chip said to the sheriff, "I'll see this gets back to Prescott as quick as I can."

He stayed in Kingman overnight and headed for home early next morning. Three days later, he crawled off his horse at the sheriff's office in Prescott and gave his report to the sheriff and handed over the money.

"You'll find that it's short one hundred and six dollars, the other guy that went South probably still has the other hundred."

The banker was elated and Chip was a big hero for a little while, then he told the sheriff he was headed for home and Becky, and when he'd had some rest and resupplied, he would head for Wickenberg and see if the other murderer was there or if they could tell him anything about him.

CHAPTER SIX

Chip sent a flying deputy to Becky saying he would be at the ranch about an hour after sundown, and have nothing on but a smile and a blanket, hot damn, he was headed home. When he got there, she was as he had requested, and they made love most of the night. When he had had enough for a while he started packing for Wickenburg, a .44 six shooter, a .44 yellow boy, serape, grub for three days, he knew Clyde would have his best horse saddled and ready to go the next morning. So he wouldn't have to waste any time getting headed out.

He got to Wickenburg late in the day, he knew there was no law office in this burg, so he headed for the livery stable, put up his horse and mosied over to the Bar Seven. The barkeep came over to his table, "say ain't you the fella that was looking for that redhead a while back?"

"Ya that was me."

"Did you find him?"

"Sure did and they hanged him in Prescott last fall."

"Are you a lawman?"

"Ya, but can you keep it under your hat for the time being, I'm a US Deputy Marshal looking for a fella that robbed the Prescott bank, killed the teller, wounded the sheriff and shot at me, he was last seen in Kingman and maybe he came this way? I don't know what he looks like, only that he's riding a L Bar L horse he stole. Have you seen anybody like that in the last week or so?"

"Ya, there was a stranger who hit town three or four days ago, you just missed him, he ate here, paid up and left, probably staying over at Mrs. Smith's boarding house."

Chip knew the man's horse was at the livery, so he ordered a meal, corned beef, mashed taters, and beans, washed it down with a strong cup of coffee. Paid the bill, retrieved the yellow boy and his pistol and walked out into the sunlight. He went over to the livery to get the bad guy's horse, he was going to saddle it and go over to Mrs. Smith's boarding house and arrest the murderer. Surprise, his horse was gone. Well hell, he'd missed him again.

"Hey oldtimer, where did that L Bar L horse go?"

"He said he was going hunting is all I know."

"Okay, thanks." That wasn't what he'd planned, but okay, he'd go over to Mrs. Smith's and see what she knew, if anything. When he got to the old rickety gate, an old colored woman was sweeping off the porch.

"Howdy, I'm looking for an acquaintance of mine, when I put my horse in the livery stable, his horse was gone, would you know where I could catch up with him?"

"Hello, I'm Mrs. Smith, and who might you be?"

"I'm Chip Colfax, can you help me?"

"You must mean Mr. Peacock, yes, he went quail hunting for me, I told him if he would bring me a big mess of birds, I would give him a free day of room and board."

"Okay, thanks, I want to surprise him, could I wait here for him?"

"That'll be alright with me, just have a seat and I'll bring you some old newspapers to read."

So Chip pulled up an old rocker and settled in for a wait, for how long he didn't know, but he would wait. Meanwhile, Mrs. Smith brought him a huge glass of lemonade and he settled in. He watched the few town folks come and go, read the old newspapers and dozed off and on. Three hours later, he noticed a lone figure coming toward the boarding house, he had a gunnysack over his shoulder as he walked along. Chip put the paper up in front of his face and waited.

Mrs. Smith opened the screen door and said, "Well Mr. Peacock, how'd you do?"

"I got thirteen quail and one six foot rattler that I shot the head off of, the birds are all field dresses and I skinned the snake."

When Peacock took the sack off his shoulder Chip was right behind him with his pistol drawn, he shoved the gun hard into his back and cocked it, "Mr. Peacock, you are under arrest for murder, bank robbery and attempted murder. Don't move or you're a dead man."

"I don't know who you are, but you are mistaken, I didn't do none of them things."

Chip took his side arm and stuck it in his belt and said, "Hands behind your back." He shackled his hands behind his back and said to Mrs. Smith, who was dumbstruck, "Mrs. Smith what time is supper, one for me and one for my prisoner."

"And oh Mr. Peacock, I'm US Deputy Marshal, Chip Colfax, now move it."

There wasn't a jail in town, but the constable, when he was around, shackled his prisoners to an old mesquite tree across from the Bar Seven, so that's what Chip did. Then he went back to the boarding house and got some food for his prisoner, then went back, got something to eat for himself. He then went to the livery and got his serape, he and Ellsworth then slept by the mesquite tree.

CHAPTER SEVEN

Chip and his prisoner left Wickenburg at daylight, he figured with hard riding, he could be back in Prescott by late afternoon, if he didn't stop at the ranch, he didn't want the murderer to know where he lived. He got into Prescott late afternoon. Gave his report to the sheriff with the leftover money, got a bite to eat, went back to the sheriff's office, wrote a message, strapped it on a Flying Deputy and sent it on its way. Message read, *Be home after dark, be ready, love Chip.*

THE END

ABOUT THE AUTHOR

Michael B. Whalen was born in Bloomington Illinois and was educated at Eureka College. He now lives in Prescott Arizona by himself, having lost his wife Dorthy after 50 years. He enjoys golf, oil painting, karaoke, and Texas hold'em. He was an electrical lineman for the power company in Arizona for 38 years.

His first book "CHIP COLFAX, YELLOW BOY RIFLE" is available at Amazon.

Prescott is in the Bradshaw Mountains with four beautiful seasons.

Made in the USA
Las Vegas, NV
21 April 2022

47770049R00020